GOING TO SCHOOL

By Rose Blake

Katrina

Frankie

Milo

Paloma

Erik

Katrina

Rose

Sonny

Alex

Jenny

Liam

Josh

Sid

Ammu

Greta

Zoe

Tommy

Frank

GOING TO SCHOOL

By Rose Blake

Lincoln
Children's Books

Today I am going to school.

My friends travel to school in lots of different ways,

but I like to ride my scooter best.

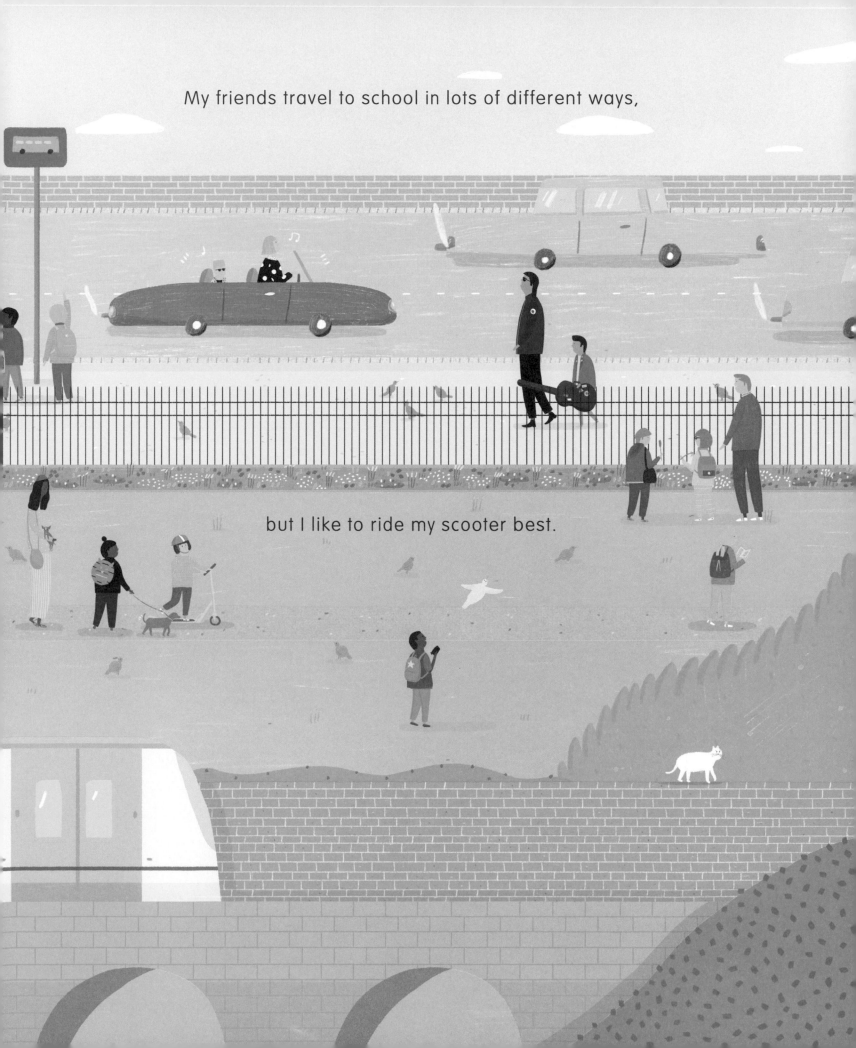

I arrive at the school gate just as the bell rings.

"Goodbye!" I say, and run inside.

This is our teacher, Miss Balmer.

"Hello!"

I hang up my coat and bag, and go inside the classroom.

geography

art

English

maths

P.E.

science

computing

drama

Miss Balmer has written what we'll be
doing today on the whiteboard.

Miss Balmer

- ✓ Katrina
- ✓ Frankie
- ✓ Milo
- ✓ Jenny
- ✓ Liam
- ✓ Josh
- ✓ Rose
- ✓ Sonny
- ✓ Alex

- ✓ Paloma
- ✓ Erik
- ✓ Grace
- ✓ Sid
- ✓ Ammu
- ✓ Greta
- Zoe
- Tommy
- Frank

At nine o'clock
we're ready to start.

Our first lesson is about
the world around us.

We learn about giant mountains and huge lakes.

Miss Balmer rolls out a map of the world, and we show each
other where some of our friends and family come from.

Art is my favourite lesson. We can make elephants out of plastic bottles,
a flock of colourful tropical birds, or a giant cardboard robot.

Today, some of us are making paper masks. Mine is a big, round moon!

The bell rings and it's break time.

In the playground, we can swing on the climbing
frame, play football, or show off our best yoyo tricks.

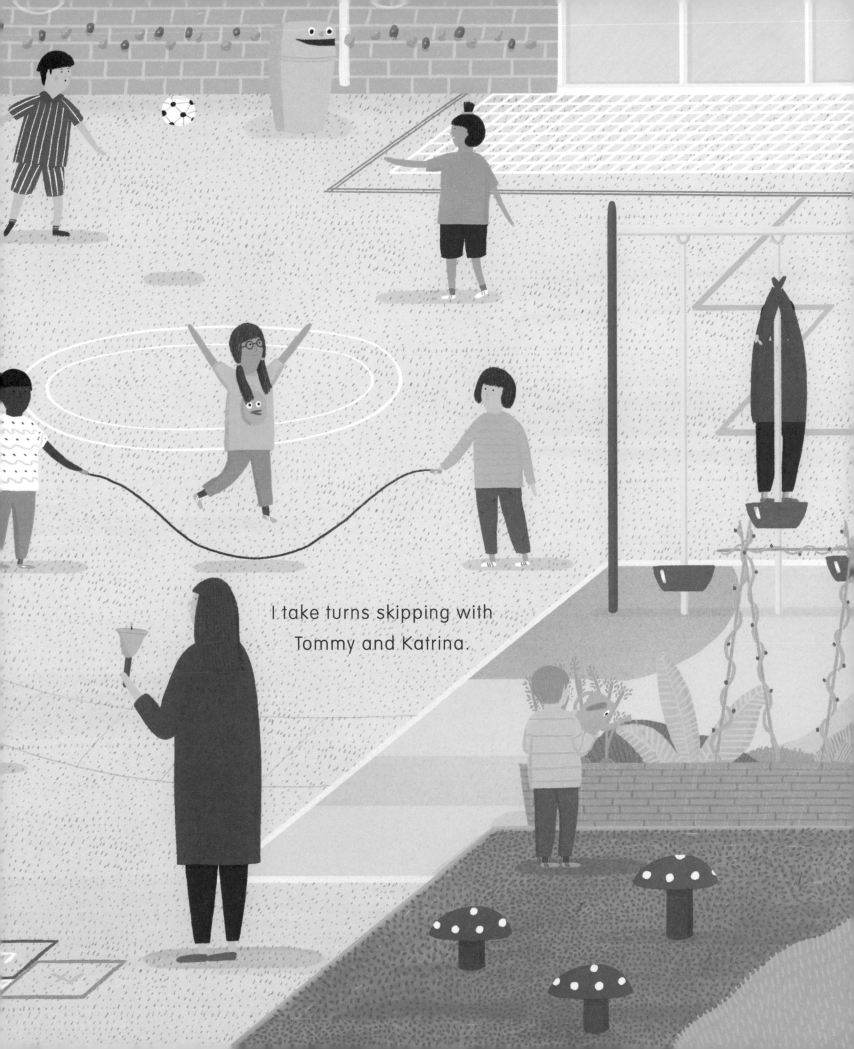

I take turns skipping with Tommy and Katrina.

After break, it's time for reading and writing. Today,
Miss Balmer is reading us a story in the Book Nook.

When I close my eyes and listen, I feel like I'm flying
through a starry sky, over a sleeping city.

Your imagination can take you to lots of exciting places when you're reading! What's your favourite story?

Then it's time for maths. We use the blocks to help us count,
solve puzzles and play fun number games.

Miss Balmer shows us how to tell the time on the clocks, and some of us play a shopping game to practise using numbers in real life.

TODAY'S SHOPPING LIST:

3 BANANAS - 10P
RED PEPPER - 70P
CHEESE - £2
2 CARROTS -
WATERMEL
6 EGGS - £1

In P.E. we put on our gym kit and run, climb, jump and stretch. Sometimes, we play team games, like football and basketball.

Greta can spin three hula hoops at a time!

Peep peep!
Miss Balmer blows
her whistle and it's
time for...

Lunch! We queue up and choose what we want to eat. I'm hungry!

I'm having chicken curry with rice, a crunchy apple... and a bar of chocolate for desert!

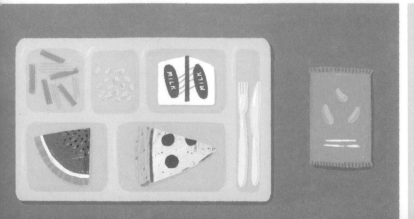

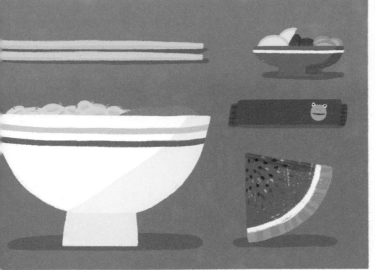

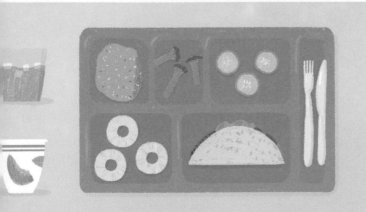

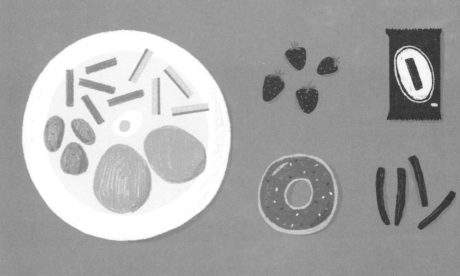

There are lots of different options to choose from. Tommy has spaghetti and a banana, and Katrina has fish, salad and an iced bun.

What do you like to eat for lunch?

After lunch we meet outside the science room and get ready for our next lesson.

There's lots to do! I check on the cress we have been growing...

CHICKS

and Frank waters the sunflowers. We are having a competition to see who can grow the tallest sunflower from a tiny seed. All you need is light and water!

Next, we spend time on the computers. I make some artwork,

but you can also play games, learn about nature, or make your own music!

The last lesson of the day is drama.
Today we're all acting out our dream jobs.

When I grow up, I want to be an artist like my Mum.

Can you tell what my friends would like to be? See if you can find any clues in the earlier lessons, too.

At the end of the afternoon,
the bell rings and it's time to go home.

Mum is waiting to pick me up at the gate.
She asks me what I did today.
"Not much," I say.

But I can't wait for tomorrow.

Going to school is great!

For P.B. and C.B. - R.B.

Brimming with creative inspiration, how-to projects, and useful information to enrich your everyday life, Quarto Knows is a favourite destination for those pursuing their interests and passions. Visit our site and dig deeper with our books into your area of interest: Quarto Creates, Quarto Cooks, Quarto Homes, Quarto Lives, Quarto Drives, Quarto Explores, Quarto Gifts, or Quarto Kids.

Going to School © 2017 Quarto Publishing plc. Text and illustrations © 2017 Rose Blake.

First published in hardback in 2017 by Lincoln Children's Books
This paperback edition first published in 2018 by Lincoln Children's Books
an imprint of The Quarto Group.
The Old Brewery, 6 Blundell Street, London N7 9BH, United Kingdom.
T (0)20 7700 6700 F (0)20 7700 8066 **www.QuartoKnows.com**

A catalogue record for this book is available from the British Library.

ISBN 978-1-78603-124-2

The illustrations were created digitally • Set in VAG rounded
Published by Rachel Williams • Designed by Nicola Price • Edited by Jenny Broom
Manufactured in Guangdong, China, CC052018

1 3 5 7 9 8 6 4 2

Swimmer

Chef

Film-maker

Vet

Fashion
Designer

Biologist

Artist

Pilot

Game
Designer

Archeologist

Policeman

Musician

Footballer

Astronaut

Teacher

Actor

Engineer

Gardener